ANIMALIA

Graeme Base

Within the pages of this book
You may discover, if you look
Beyond the spell of written words,
A hidden land of beasts and birds.

For many things are 'of a kind',
And those with keenest eyes will find
A thousand things, or maybe more —
It's up to you to keep the score.

A final word before we go;
There's one more thing you ought to know:
In Animalia, you see,
It's possible you might find *me*.

— Graeme

For Robyn

Abrams Books for Young Readers, New York

Copyright © Graeme Base, 1986   A Robert Sessions Book

This 1993 edition published by Abrams Books for Young Readers, an imprint of ABRAMS.

Abrams Books for Young Readers are available at special discounts when purchased in quantity for premiums
and promotions as well as fundraising or educational use. Special editions can also be created to specification.
For details, contact specialsales@abramsbooks.com or the address below.

ABRAMS
THE ART OF BOOKS SINCE 1949

115 West 18th Street
New York, NY 10011
www.abramsbooks.com

Printed and Bound in China
18 17

ISBN: 978-0-8109-1939-6

An Armoured Armadillo Avoiding An Angry Alligator

Beautiful BLUE BUTTERFLIES basking by a BABBLING BROOK

Crafty Crimson Cats care

GREAT GREEN GORILLAS
GROWING GRAPES IN A
GORGEOUS GLASS GREENHOUSE

Horrible hairy hogs

hurrying
home-
-ward

on

heavily-
harnessed
horses

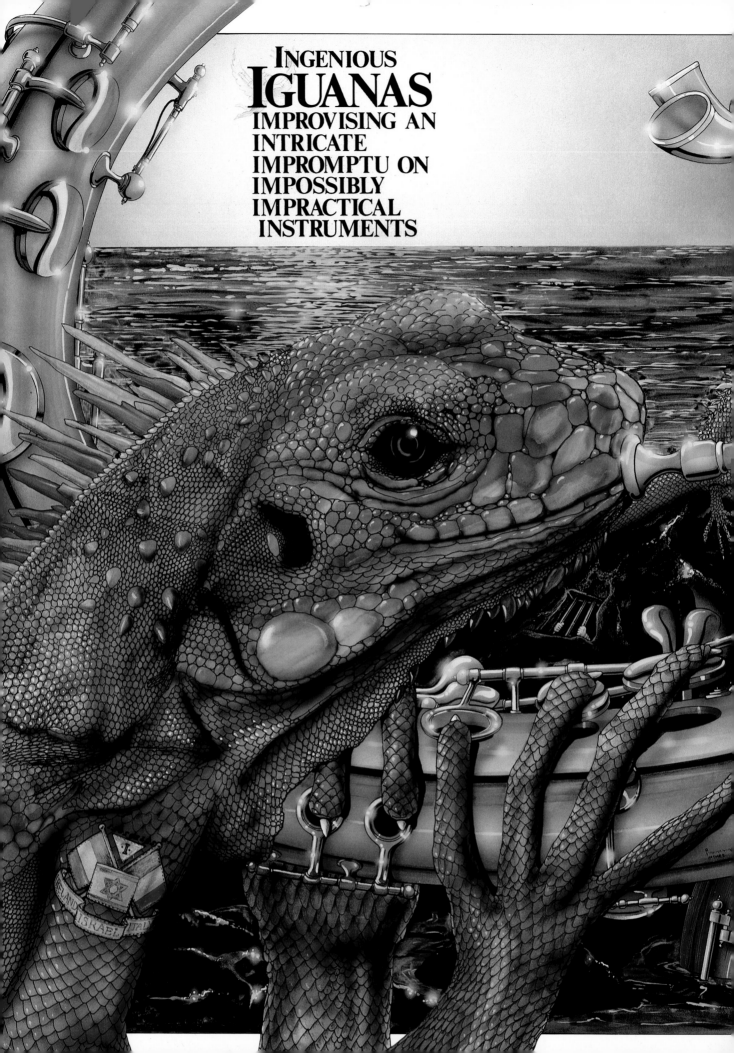

INGENIOUS IGUANAS
IMPROVISING AN INTRICATE IMPROMPTU ON IMPOSSIBLY IMPRACTICAL INSTRUMENTS

JOVIAL · JACKALS · JUGGLING · JUGS · OF · JELLY · IN · THE · JUNGLE

Nine Nautical Newts
Navigating
Near Norway

ONE
OUTRAGEOUS
OLD
OSTRICH
ORDERING
AN
ONION
OMELETTE

Proud Peacocks

Preening Perfect Plumage

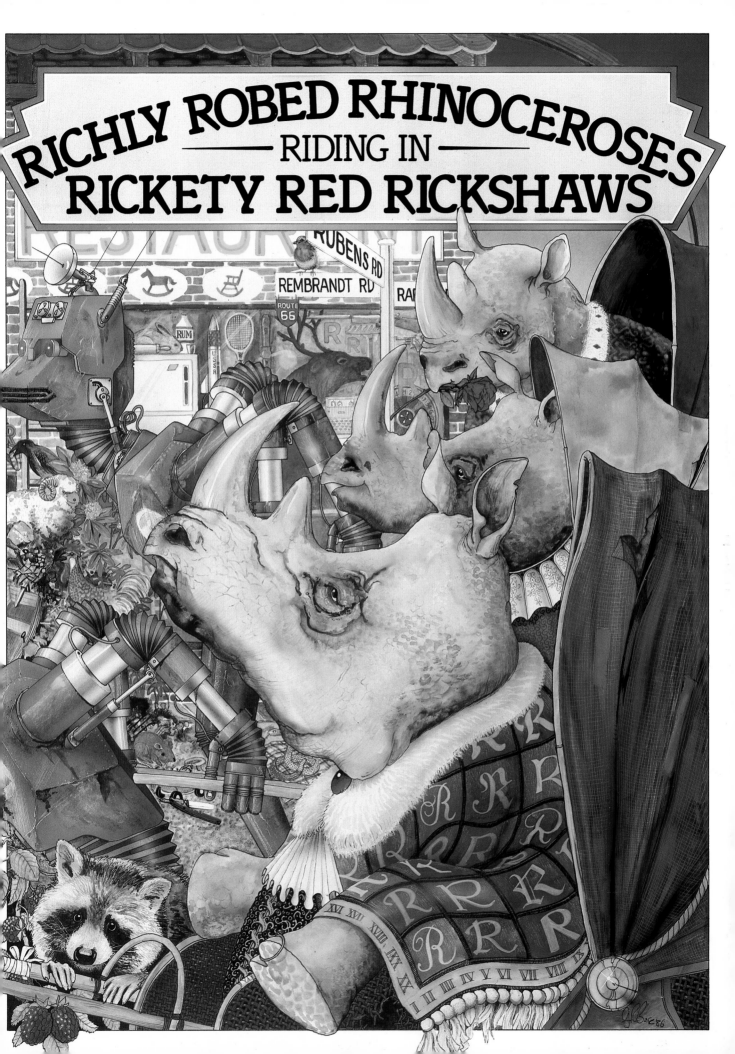

TWO TIGERS TAKING THE 10.20 TRAIN TO TIMBUKTU

UNRULY UNICORNS UPENDING URNS OF ULTRAMARINE UMBRELLAS

Wicked
Warrior
WASPS
wildly
waving
Warlike
Weapons

YOUTHFUL YAKS YODELLING
IN YELLOW YACHTS

Z.
ZANY ZEBRAS ZIGZAGGING IN ZINC ZEPPELINS

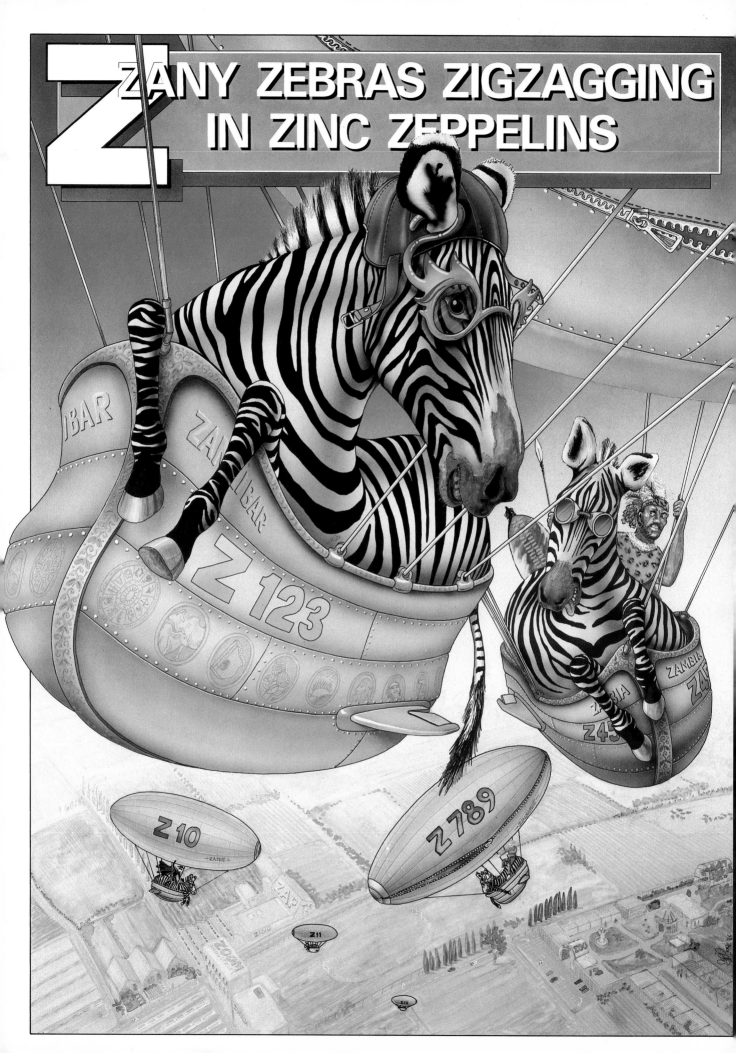